P9-DGR-368

GO TO BED, MONSTER!

Written by Natasha Wing

Illustrated by Sylvie Kantorovitz

Harcourt, Inc.

Orlando Austin New York San Diego Toronto London

Text copyright © 2007 by Natasha Wing
Illustrations copyright © 2007 by Sylvie Kantorovitz

All rights reserved. No part of this publication may be reproduced or transmitted
in any form or by any means, electronic or mechanical, including photocopy, recording, or any information
storage and retrieval system, without permission in writing from the publisher.

Requests for permission to make copies of any part of the work should be submitted online
at www.harcourt.com/contact or mailed to the following address: Permissions Department,
Harcourt, Inc., 6277 Sea Harbor Drive, Orlando, Florida 32887-6777.

www.HarcourtBooks.com

Library of Congress Cataloging-in-Publication Data
Wing, Natasha.
Go to bed, Monster! / Natasha Wing; illustrated by Sylvie Kantorovitz.
p. cm.
Summary: Trying to avoid bedtime, Lucy uses her imagination
and some crayons to draw a monster to play with.
[1. Imagination—Fiction. 2. Drawing—Fiction. 3. Monsters—Fiction. 4. Bedtime—Fiction.]
I. Kantorovitz, Sylvie, ill. II. Title.
PZ7.W72825Go 2007
[E]—dc22 2006010849
ISBN 978-0-15-205775-6

First edition
A C E G H F D B

Printed in Singapore

The illustrations in this book were done in oil paints and oil pastels on primed paper.
The display type and text type were set in Potato Cut.
Color separations by Colourscan Co. Pte. Ltd., Singapore
Printed and bound by Tien Wah Press, Singapore
Production supervision by Christine Witnik
Designed by Lydia D'moch

R0413039559

To the creative monster within—may you never go to sleep.
—N. W.

To Samantha, my drawing monster. With love.
— S. K.

One night, Lucy tossed and turned.
She could not, would not, did not
want to go to bed.
"I want to draw," she said.

Lucy dumped out her crayons.
She drew an oval body. A square head.
Rectangle legs. And circle eyes.

When she added triangles,

the shapes
turned into a . . .

ROAR!

said Monster.

"You don't scare me," said Lucy.
"Let's play!"

Lucy and Monster built castles.

They flew airplanes.

They marched in a parade.

Then they skipped

and jumped

and crawled

and stomped

until Lucy was
all worn out.

"Let's play sleeping lions,"
said Lucy.

CHASE!

roared Monster.

"I'm too tired," said Lucy.
"And so are you.
Go to bed."

Lucy drew Monster a bed.
But Monster would not go to bed.

Garrrrrr rr

HUNGRY

roared Monster.

Lucy drew a mountain of meatballs.

Glub

Glub

Lucy drew a bucket of water.

Lucy drew a bathroom.

MORE PLAY?

asked Monster.

"Go to bed," moaned Lucy.

But Monster would not go to bed.

"COLD" whined Monster.

Lucy drew pajamas.

Lucy drew a huggy bear.

DARK

Lucy drew a moon.

Then Lucy crossed her arms.
"That's enough. Now go to bed."

NOT SLEEPY

snapped Monster.

"Maybe this will help,"
said Lucy.

BOOK!

cheered Monster.

"Only if you get into bed," said Lucy.

Monster climbed into bed.

SOFT

sighed Monster.

Lucy tucked in Monster.
Then she read and read and read.

SLEEPY

whispered Monster.

Lucy watched one circle eye,
then two circle eyes, slowly
close.

Lucy drew curtains over the moon.

She laid down her head.

Then she finally,
peacefully,
went to sleep.